Little
Thumb

Little
Thumb

Written by Wanda Dionne

Illustrated by Jana Dillon

PELICAN PUBLISHING COMPANY
Gretna 2001

The Author's Dedication:

To all the little people who gather comfort and courage by sucking their thumbs—
and to all the big people who love them

With special acknowledgments to my mentor, Guida Jackson,
who would not allow me to lose faith,
and to Patricia Pennington Malcolm,
who sparked the idea for this book

The Illustrator's Dedication:

To Elizabeth Stock, my model for the illustrations,
and to her parents, Diane and Tim, her brothers Tim and Stephen,
and her grandmother Ethel Brown, wonderful neighbors all

The word "Pelican" and the depiction of a pelican
are trademarks of Pelican Publishing Company, Inc., and are registered
in the U.S. Patent and Trademark Office.

Library of Congress Cataloging-in-Publication Data

Dionne, Wanda
    Little thumb / written by Wanda Dionne ; illustrated by Jana Dillon.
        p. cm.
    Summary: Little Thumb recounts rhyming reasons why it really should not go into its owner's mouth.
    ISBN 1-56554-754-3 (hc. : alk. paper)
    [1. Thumb sucking—Fiction. 2. Stories in rhyme.] I. Dillon, Jana, ill. II. Title.

PZ8.3.D5993 Li 2000
[E]—dc21

                                                                    99-056098

Printed in Hong Kong

Published by Pelican Publishing Company, Inc.
1000 Burmaster Street, Gretna, Louisiana 70053

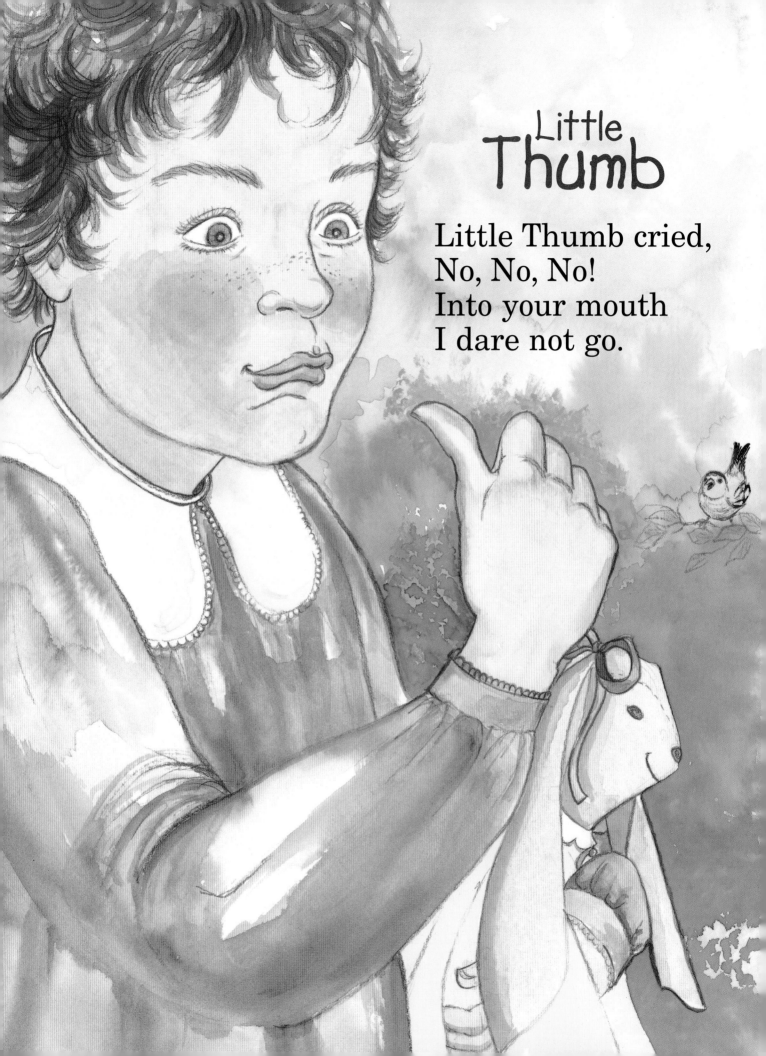

Little
Thumb

Little Thumb cried,
No, No, No!
Into your mouth
I dare not go.

It's scary and **dark**,
And damp like a cave.
Don't make me go.
I'm not at all brave.

You've got small white teeth,
That chew and that bite.

A roller-coaster tongue.
Oh! What a fright!

There are scary sounds, too,
When you swallow or slurp.

The motion makes me shiver
When you hiccup or burp.

I can carry bad germs
That will make you sick.
I'm not clean, I'm dirty—
I'm not safe to lick.

Besides . . .
Little Thumb cried,
I want so much more!
Don't hide me, or bite me,
Or make my nail sore.

The skin on my backside
Has lines and whorls,
That make us different
From the rest of the world.

Look closely at me
And think of YOU.
Count all the great things
That we can do.

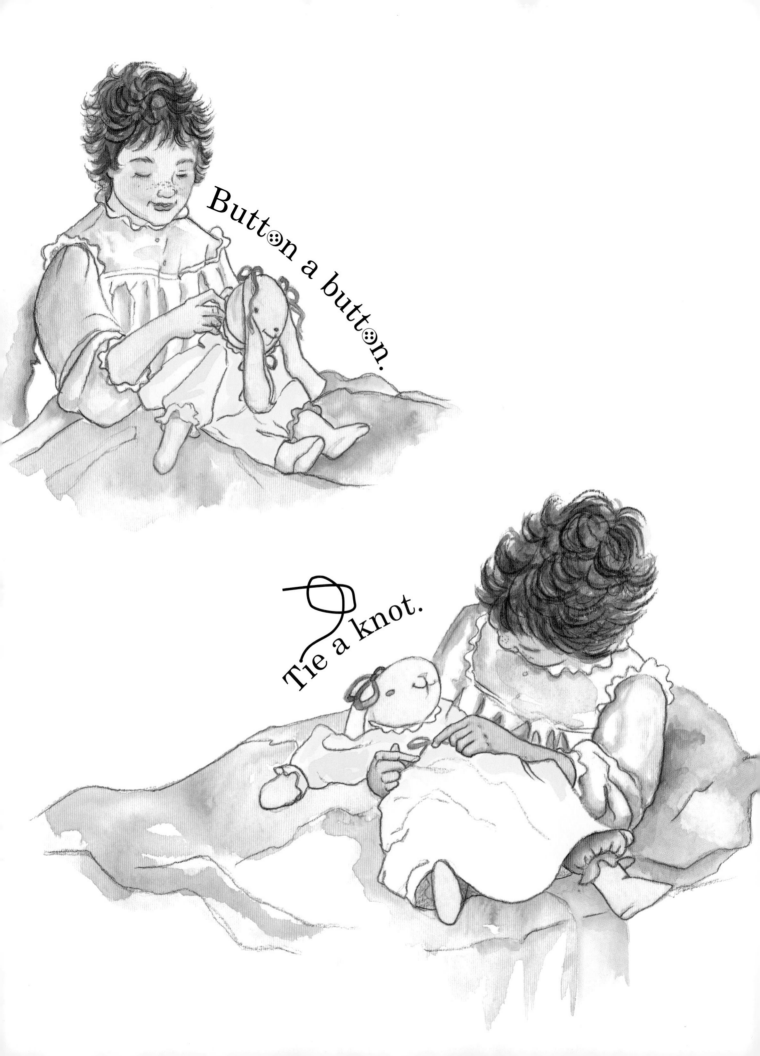

Button a button.

Tie a knot.

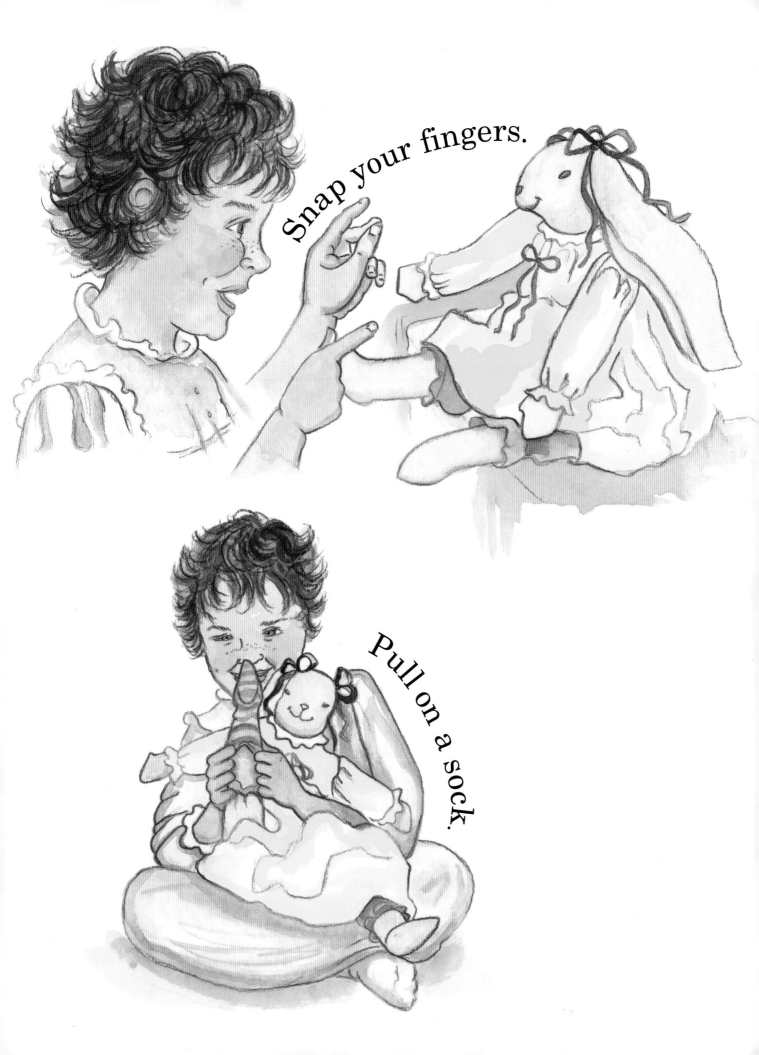

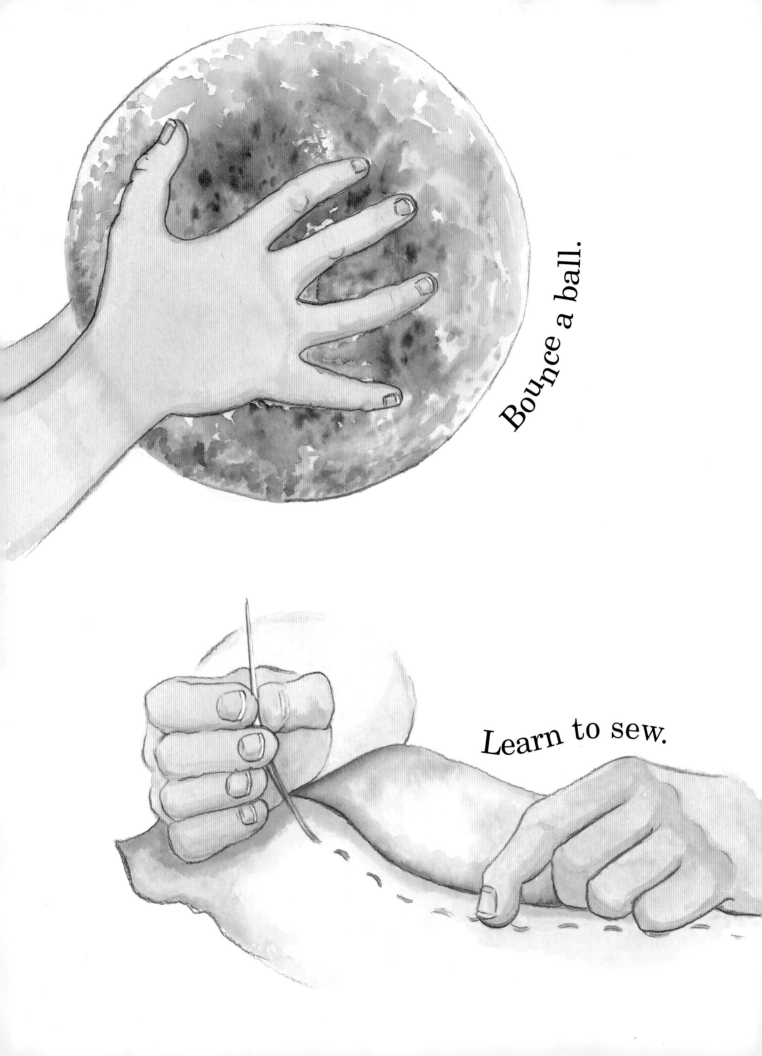

Bounce a ball.

Learn to sew.

Pick up sticks.

Way to go!

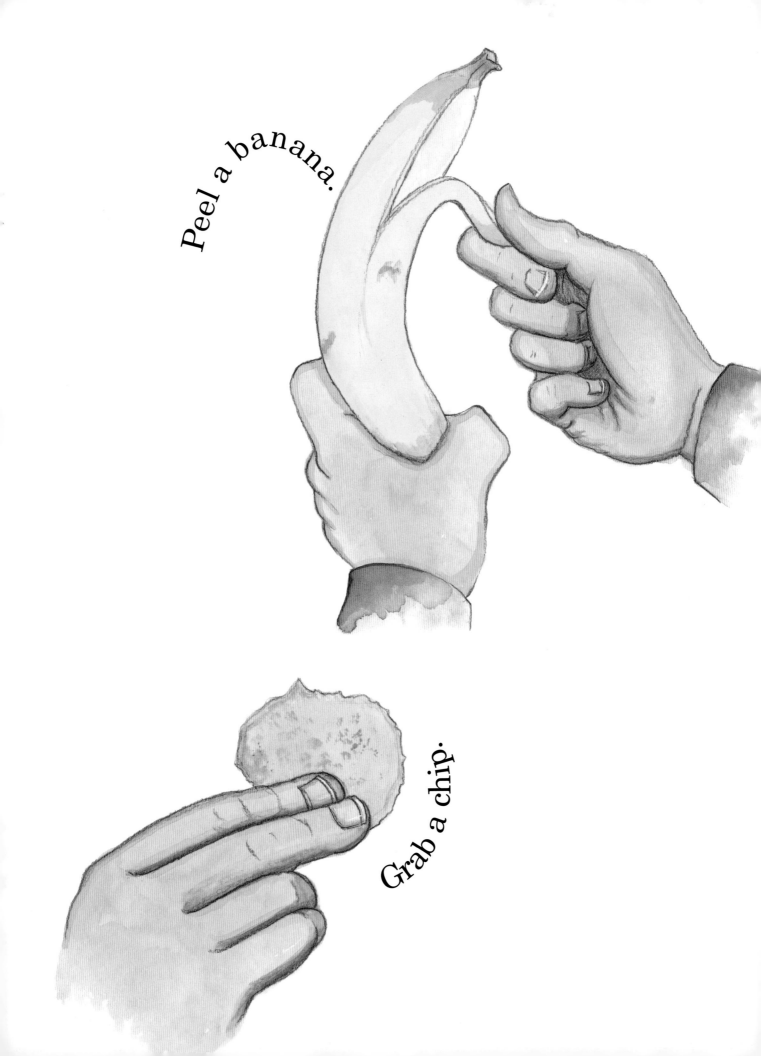

Peel a banana.

Grab a chip.

Hold a sandwich.

Get a grip!

Pull or pry.
Pinch or tug.

Pet and prod.
Tickle and hug.

Turn a knob.
Open a door.
If you put your mind to it,
We can do so much more.

Flowers to pick.
Pebbles to throw.
Mud pies to make.
Gardens to grow.

Go to "big school."
Learn how to write.

SCHOOL BUS

Ride on a bus—
Hold on tight.

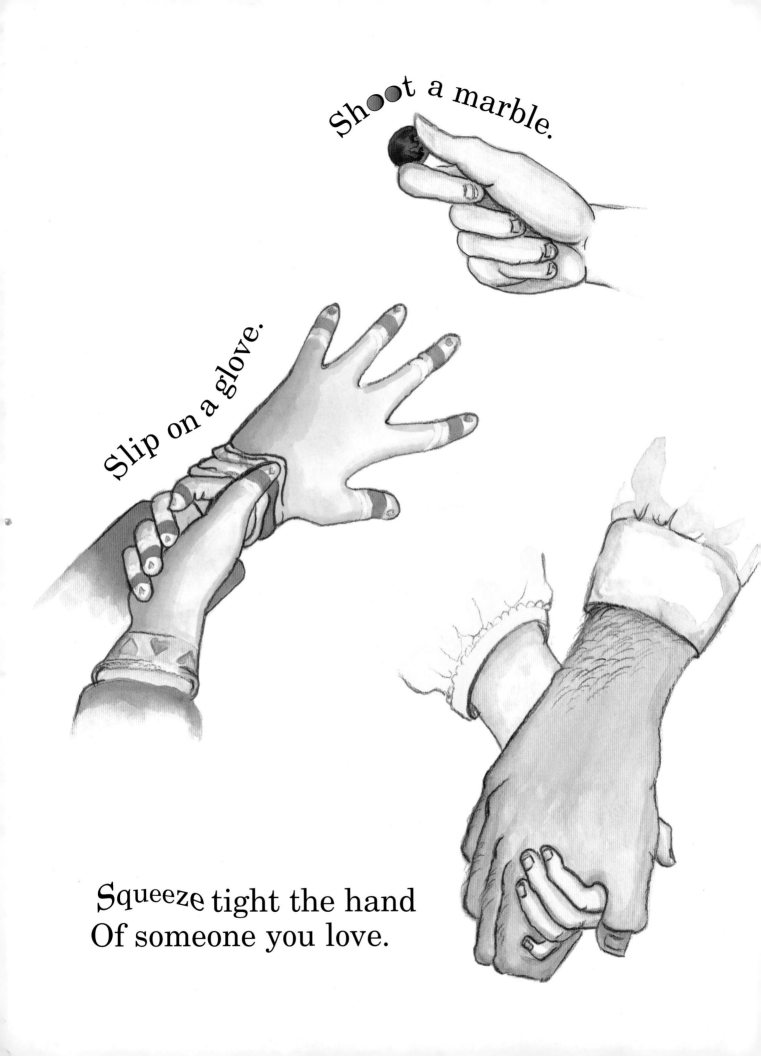

Sh**oo**t a marble.

Slip on a glove.

Squeeze tight the hand
Of someone you love.

I want to be outside,
Not out of sight.
I want to do fun things
In the warm sunlight.

So out of your mouth
Let Thumb stay and play!
That way we'll both
Have a wonderful day!